I0797545

INSIDE MLS

LOS ANGELES FOOTBALL CLUB

BY CHRÖS MCDOUGALL

SportsZone
An Imprint of Abdo Publishing
abdobooks.com

abdobooks.com

Published by Abdo Publishing, a division of ABDO, PO Box 398166, Minneapolis, Minnesota 55439.

Printed in the United States of America, North Mankato, Minnesota
052021
092021

Cover Photo: Jon Endow/Image of Sport/AP Images
Interior Photos: Ed Ruvalcaba/Image of Sport/AP Images, 5, 8, 32; Scott Winters/Icon Sportswire/AP Images, 7; Jon Endow/Image of Sport/AP Images, 10; Javier Rojas/Pi/Zuma Press/Newscom, 12; AP Images, 15; Ric Francis/AP Images, 17; Stephen Carr/Press-Telegram/AP Images, 18; Nick Ut/AP Images, 21; Jevone Moore/Cal Sport Media/AP Images, 22; Reed Saxon/AP Images, 25; Kyusung Gong/Icon Sportswire/AP Images, 27, 43; Chris Carlson/AP Images, 29; Peter Joneleit/Icon Sportswire/AP Images, 31; Ringo H.W. Chiu/AP Images, 35; Marcio Jose Sanchez/AP Images, 37, 41; Jae C. Hong/AP Images, 38

Editor: Patrick Donnelly
Series Designer: Dan Peluso

Library of Congress Control Number: 2020948259

Publisher's Cataloging-in-Publication Data

Names: McDougall, Chrös, author.
Title: Los Angeles Football Club / by Chrös McDougall
Description: Minneapolis, Minnesota : Abdo Publishing, 2022 | Series: Inside MLS | Includes online resources and index.
Identifiers: ISBN 9781532194740 (lib. bdg.) | ISBN 9781098214401 (ebook)
Subjects: LCSH: Soccer teams--Juvenile literature. | Professional sports franchises--Juvenile literature. | Sports Teams--Juvenile literature.
Classification: DDC 796.334--dc23

TABLE OF CONTENTS

CHAPTER 1

BEST SEASON EVER

Fans stood at their seats in Banc of California Stadium. A national audience tuned in on TV. One year earlier, Los Angeles Football Club (LAFC) had reached the playoffs in its first Major League Soccer (MLS) season. Now the team was looking to do even better. The 2019 season wasn't off to the best start, though.

Sporting Kansas City was in town for the season opener on March 3. The visitors took an early 1–0 lead, but Diego Rossi tied it up for LAFC just after halftime. And that's how it stayed. Fans watched as the 90th minute expired. One minute of stoppage time passed. Then another. The hotly anticipated 2019 season was looking sure to start with an uninspiring draw.

Diego Rossi, left, *scored the first goal of the season for LAFC in 2019.*

YouTube TV

That's when the ball arrived at Adama Diomande's feet. The Norwegian forward cut inside. Two defenders were still moving the other direction. Diomande tapped the ball once. Then he squared up and drilled a right-footed shot from just inside the penalty area. Sporting KC's goalkeeper could only flail his body. The ball was already past him on the way to the back of the net.

Diomande's 94th-minute goal secured a 2–1 win to kick off LAFC's season. And for the second-year club, the winning was only just getting started.

ONWARD WE GO

LAFC went on to win again the next weekend. Then, after a 2–2 draw on the road with New York City Football Club (FC), Los Angeles won its next four games. By June 1, the team was 11–1–4 and building a huge lead in the Western Conference.

Few were surprised about LAFC's hot start. Its 2018 season was one of the best ever by an MLS expansion team. The team had a proven leader in Bob Bradley, one of the league's most respected coaches. Carlos Vela, meanwhile, led a lethal offense. In his first MLS season in 2018, he scored 14 goals with 13 assists. It soon became clear that the 2019 LAFC team wasn't just good, though. It had the potential to be historically good.

Head coach Bob Bradley proved to be the right man for the job in Los Angeles.

On August 21, LAFC beat the San Jose Earthquakes 4–0 at home. That gave the team a record of 19–3–4, good for 61 points. The next-best team in the Western Conference was 19 back. Even the Eastern Conference leader trailed Los Angeles

LAFC players celebrate after clinching the MLS Supporters' Shield in just the club's second season.

by 16 points. The Supporters' Shield, given to the best team in the MLS regular season, was almost a certainty for LAFC—and the season still had two months to go.

One huge reason for that success was Vela. In his second MLS season, the crafty forward became a force. His two goals against San Jose were his 25th and 26th of the season. No MLS player had more. Vela was hardly the only LAFC player thriving, though. Fellow forward Rossi was a dangerous attacking threat in his own right. Midfielders Mark-Anthony Kaye and Eduard Atuesta and defender Walker Zimmerman were enjoying breakout seasons as well. At their best, the Black and Gold simply dismantled opponents. They would methodically break down opposing defenses. And when the other team got the ball, LAFC would swarm to quickly win it back.

A little more than a month later, on September 25, LAFC clinched the Supporters' Shield with a 3–1 win over the Houston Dynamo. However, by then the team was sputtering a bit. The victory over Houston was the team's first in six games. Amidst that stretch was a 2–0 loss to Minnesota United—LAFC's first home defeat of 2019. Then Los Angeles followed up the Houston win with a 1–1 draw at Minnesota. Just a few weeks earlier, LAFC appeared certain to break the MLS single-season record of 71 points. But going into the final game of the season, it had 69. Only a win against the Colorado Rapids would do.

DECISION DAY

The afternoon sun shone down on Banc of California Stadium.

THE NORTH END

From the start LAFC fans have been known for creating one of the most exciting atmospheres in MLS. The loudest fans sit in the North End of the team's home stadium. They are part of the 3252, which organizes hardcore fans and supporters' groups. They're not the only ones passionate about LAFC, though. Before COVID-19 disrupted the 2020 season, the team had sold out every home game.

Fan support was amazing from the start for LAFC.

LAFC's fans, already known as some of the loudest and most energetic in the league, had the stadium rocking. Now their team needed to take care of business.

In the 28th minute, Vela got the ball 10 yards out of the Rapids' penalty area. Two defenders dropped back to stop him from advancing. That was a bad idea. Using his free space, Vela lined up and drilled a left-footed shot. The ball curved through the air and past Rapids goalkeeper Tim Howard into the top left corner. Vela's 32nd goal of the year set the MLS single-season record. And he was only getting started.

Three minutes later, a lobbed cross found LAFC's Tristan Blackmon to the right of Colorado's goal. He headed the ball toward the front of the net, where it skipped past Vela. But Vela didn't give up on the play. Turning his body, he patiently waited for the perfect moment. Then he went airborne, falling backwards while swinging his legs, perfectly striking the ball for a bicycle kick into the net.

Although Colorado got a goal back just before halftime, this was going to be LAFC's day. In the 51st minute, Blackmon found Vela again to complete the hat trick. Both players broke free from their defenders, and Vela tapped in the crossing ball while on the run to seal the 3–1 win.

Carlos Vela's bicycle kick was part of his record-setting hat trick against the Colorado Rapids on the final day of the 2019 regular season.

It marked the perfect way to finish a special season—both for Vela and for LAFC. Vela ended the season with an MLS record 34 goals, to go along with his 15 assists. He was later named the league's Most Valuable Player (MVP). LAFC, meanwhile, finished the season with 72 points. That eclipsed the record of 71 set one year earlier by the New York Red Bulls. That's not all, though. LAFC's 85 goals tied the MLS record set in 1998 by the LA Galaxy, and their plus-48 goal differential bettered that Galaxy team's record of plus-41.

Howard, who was playing in the last top-level game of his 21-year career, came away impressed. "That LAFC team is not like many I've ever seen," he said. "They're very good."

CHAMPIONS LEAGUE

LAFC's dominant 2019 season earned the team a berth in the next year's Concacaf Champions League. That tournament features the best teams from North America, Central America, and the Caribbean. Play was suspended midway through the tournament due to COVID-19. When it came back, LAFC continued to roll, advancing all the way to the final. LAFC became only the fourth MLS team to reach the final in the current format of the tournament that began in 2009. Diego Rossi then put LAFC up just after halftime against Tigres UANL of Mexico. However, Tigres came back to win 2–1.

CHAPTER 2

LA SOCCER

There was little reason for celebration on the afternoon of October 26, 2014, in Carson, California. In a stadium that routinely drew crowds of more than 21,000 for Galaxy games, Chivas USA and the San Jose Earthquakes kicked off in front of a sea of empty green seats. Nothing was at stake in the contest between two of MLS' worst teams. And after Félix Borja's goal secured a 1–0 win for Chivas USA, one of the great experiments in American pro soccer was over.

Before Los Angeles was the center of the world's entertainment industry, and before it was even a sprawling metropolis, people in the city were playing soccer. In the early 1900s, they were mostly immigrants. Eventually, pro soccer began to take hold.

Former Manchester United star George Best was one of the European stars who played for the Los Angeles Aztecs.

11

The North American Soccer League began in 1968. From 1974 until folding in 1981, the Los Angeles Aztecs had spurts of success featuring world-famous stars such as George Best and Johan Cruyff.

The area became a soccer hub in other ways, too. It hosted three World Cup finals—1994 for the men, and 1999 and 2003 for the women—as well as the 1984 Olympic men's gold medal match. Major teams from around the world routinely come to the city to play friendlies. And since MLS began in 1996, the LA Galaxy have been one of the league's most popular teams. However, all of that soccer history was not enough to make Chivas USA work.

CHIVAS IN THE USA

MLS played its first season in 1996, just two years after the United States hosted the men's World Cup for the first time. Interest in the game was at an all-time high. By 2002, however, some MLS teams were struggling. The league had to shut down the Tampa Bay Mutiny and Miami Fusion. Many questioned if the entire league might follow.

Instead, MLS began rebuilding. And in 2005, it started growing again with the addition of two teams: Real Salt Lake

Hopes ran high when head coach Thomas Rongen and Chivas USA joined MLS, but success was fleeting for the expansion club.

Brad Guzan played goalkeeper for Chivas USA from 2005 to 2008.

and Chivas USA. Real Salt Lake was starting from scratch like a typical expansion team. Chivas USA was a little different.

Club Deportivo Guadalajara, often known as Chivas de Guadalajara, is one of Mexico's most popular teams. Los Angeles has a large Latino population, including many Mexican Americans. The Galaxy, meanwhile, had just opened a brand new soccer-specific stadium in nearby Carson in 2003. So Chivas de Guadalajara created a sister team in MLS called Chivas USA. The team would share a similar look with the Mexican club and share the stadium with the Galaxy. It hoped to reach a Latino fanbase that MLS was struggling to connect with.

Chivas USA had some bright spots on the field. The team, known as the Goats, reached the playoffs in just its second season. In 2007 it had the best record in the Western Conference. Among the standout players were US national team stars Brad Guzan, Sacha Kljestan, and Jonathan Bornstein. Coach Bob Bradley guided the team for one season. He would go on to lead the US team and later LAFC.

However, Chivas USA struggled mightily off the field. Early on the team's marketing efforts mainly targeted Latin American fans. This meant it was overlooking a lot of other potential fans. As a result, the team never had great fan backing. Chivas USA's existing support dipped as the on-field struggles mounted. After making the playoffs four years in a row from 2006 to 2009, Chivas USA never got back.

What really doomed the team, though, was an ownership change in 2012. The club was so poorly managed that MLS took control of it in 2014. After playing in front of home crowds averaging just over 7,000 that season, the team's fate was clear by the time it hosted the Earthquakes in the season finale. Chivas USA shut down the next day. However, plans were already in place to bring a second team back to Los Angeles.

BECOMING LAFC

Around the world, some of the most famous soccer rivalries are between teams that play in the same city. Those in charge of MLS never gave up the dream of Los Angeles having two teams. In fact, just days after Chivas USA folded, the league had announced a replacement was coming.

SUPERCLASICO

One part of Chivas USA's history that carried over to LAFC was the rivalry with the Galaxy. Many of Chivas USA's most memorable games came against the Galaxy. However, Chivas didn't have much success in the rivalry, which was called the SuperClasico. The Galaxy won the all-time series 22–4 with 8 draws.

The league was determined to not make the same mistakes with the new team that it had with Chivas USA. It sought to find wealthy, local owners who would put a lot of resources into the team. MLS wanted the team to have its own home stadium, separate from the Galaxy. And the new team would be for all of Los Angeles, not just certain groups.

Soon those pieces started coming into place. Over the coming

MLS Commissioner Don Garber, *second from right*, is flanked by LAFC's new owners as the league announced the birth of its newest club in October 2014.

years, the ownership group grew to include more than 30 people. Among them were popular local celebrities, including former US soccer star Mia Hamm, Lakers legend Magic Johnson, and actor Will Ferrell.

In September 2015, the new team got its name: Los Angeles Football Club. LAFC turned to its fans to help decide what the new team would look like. The following January, the colors

Banc of California Stadium was a state-of-the-art facility built to host LAFC matches.

ANGEL CITY FC

Pro women's soccer began to emerge in the United States during the early 2000s. Two leagues came and went before the National Women's Soccer League brought stability in 2013. Yet for all of Los Angeles' success with pro men's soccer, the city had just one season with a pro women's team. The Sol, featuring Brazilian star Marta, folded after their lone season in 2009. Angel City FC is aiming to change that. A group of celebrities and former athletes founded the team in 2020. It planned to debut in 2022, playing home games at Banc of California Stadium.

were revealed as "Pitch Black" and "California Gold." The team's crest was shaped like the seal of the city. On the logo, a wing paid tribute to Los Angeles' nickname, the "City of Angels."

"I hope our supporters here and the people of the city will wear it proudly," managing partner Henry Nguyen said. "To us it not only represents our club, it represents our city."

The last big task to check off was a stadium. In 2016, construction began in Exposition Park, a region located beside Los Angeles Memorial Coliseum in the heart of the city. Two years later, Banc of California Stadium opened in April 2018. At a cost of $350 million and with seating for 22,000 fans, it was instantly one of the country's finest soccer stadiums. Already 17,500 season tickets had been sold. Now all that was left was to get on the field and start playing some games.

CHAPTER 3

BLACK AND GOLD STARS

A person's head, wearing an LAFC cap and looking down, appeared on the screen. Slowly, he looked up and straight into the camera. It was Bob Bradley, the first coach of LAFC.

Bradley was the first of many people LAFC would introduce in this way. This July 27, 2017, announcement was especially important, though. Los Angeles already was home to MLS' most successful team, the Galaxy. Fans would need a reason to support LAFC instead. One way the team aimed to do that was by fielding a star-studded, competitive team in its first season. The Black and Gold hadn't signed any players yet. In hiring Bradley, though, the team showed it was serious.

Head coach Bob Bradley was the center of attention at the first LAFC training camp.

@LAFC
FOOTBALL CLUB
LOS ANGELES
FOOTBALL CLUB
ANGELES
BALL CLUB
LOS ANGELES
FOOTBALL CLUB
LA
52
MLS
KCAL 9

The veteran Bradley was one of the most accomplished American coaches of all time. He had led the US men's national team to the round of 16 at the 2010 World Cup. He later coached the Egyptian men's national team and pro men's teams in Norway, France, and Great Britain. Importantly, he had also been successful in MLS. That included leading the Chicago Fire to the 1998 MLS Cup in their first season.

The no-nonsense coach from New Jersey quickly began living up to LAFC's high expectations. When the team finally signed some players, Bradley installed an aggressive playing style. Using that approach, LAFC marched to the third-best record in the Western Conference in 2018. One year later, Bradley guided the team to the best record in MLS history. Afterward, he was named the league's Coach of the Year for the third time.

JUST SAY VELA

Los Angeles is a city that loves winners. It's also a city that embraces its superstars. No team has proven this more than basketball's Lakers. Star players such as Magic Johnson and Kobe Bryant won championships and became icons in the city. For LAFC to truly become Los Angeles' team, it would need a superstar of its own. On August 10, 2017, it got one.

Carlos Vela was LAFC's first captain and first superstar.

That day Carlos Vela, one of Mexico's best players and in the prime of his career, became LAFC's first Designated Player (DP). That meant his high salary would fall mostly outside the league's salary cap. He proved to be worth every dollar. Vela led LAFC in scoring in 2018, despite missing some games to play in the World Cup. Then he set the league's single-season scoring record while winning the MLS MVP award in 2019.

Just as importantly, the city embraced the humble superstar. A 2020 poll asked locals to name the city's most popular athlete. The Lakers' LeBron James, one of the best basketball players of all time, finished first. Cody Bellinger of the Dodgers, one of baseball's classic teams, came in second. And third was Vela, a player whose team had only existed for two seasons.

LAFC had reason to expect that might happen. Vela, a native of Cancun, first made his name on Mexico's youth national teams. He made his World Cup debut in 2010. Since 2011, he had been playing club soccer for Real Sociedad in Spain. It was at LAFC, however, where he truly blossomed into a superstar. His mix of creativity and technical ability allowed him to quickly become one of MLS' most dominant players ever. And Los Angeles, a city with a large Mexican American population, was quick to embrace him as their own.

In 2019 Vela became the first Mexican player to be named MLS MVP.

WORLD CUP

Sometimes having great players can create new challenges. Early in the 2018 season, LAFC had to carry on without four of its key players. They had left to play for their national teams in the World Cup in Russia. Carlos Vela helped Mexico reach the knockout round. Marco Ureña (Costa Rica) and Omar Gaber (Egypt) were eliminated in the group stage. And after training with Belgium, Laurent Ciman was cut just before the tournament.

Vela was a natural star, a perfect fit for a city with a history of supporting flashy celebrities and athletes. He was able to do things on the field that left even teammates in awe.

"It's hard for us to put it into words because we've never seen something like that," LAFC keeper Tyler Miller said after one game. After his record-setting 2019 season, however, Vela knew he still needed to do more.

"This (MVP) trophy just makes me more hungry," he said. "The next step is to be champion. I will work really hard to get that trophy for my team, for my club. This one is just OK. I want the bigger one."

STARS ALL AROUND

Not long after signing Vela, the team announced it was bringing in a young forward from Uruguay to be its second DP. Nineteen-year-old Diego Rossi didn't have Vela's fame. It didn't

Midfielder Mark-Anthony Kaye, *left*, and defender Jordan Harvey celebrate an LAFC goal.

take long for him to show he was a worthy strike partner, though. On March 4, 2018, the 5-foot-7 attacker took a pass from Vela and blasted a long shot past the Seattle Sounders goalie. It marked the first goal in LAFC history. Rossi would go on to score 12 that season and add 16 more in 2019. He took on an even bigger role in 2020. With the league in turmoil due to COVID-19 and Vela missing much of the season due to injury, Rossi stepped up and scored an MLS-best 14 goals in the shortened season. At 22, he became the youngest player to lead the league in goals. It was little surprise when he was then named MLS' first Young Player of the Year, given to the best player 22 or under.

Eddie Segura was a big part of LAFC's back line in 2019.

The team also got eight goals that season from veteran Bradley Wright-Phillips. He had been one of MLS' most potent goal-scorers while with the New York Red Bulls. After battling through injuries in 2019 with New York, the 35-year-old striker was named MLS' 2020 Comeback Player of the Year in his lone season with LAFC.

Over the years, the team's attackers usually had strong support in the midfield. Mark-Anthony Kaye of Canada, Eduard Atuesta of Colombia, and Latif Blessing of Ghana were among the team's standouts in its early years.

With all of that offensive firepower, LAFC's defense was sometimes overlooked. But only 10 teams allowed fewer goals in 2018. No team was as stingy in 2019. Belgian star Laurent Ciman was a key cog in that first LAFC team. Center back Walker Zimmerman and goalie Miller were key players the first two seasons. By 2020, all three were gone. The team took a step back defensively, but with Eddie Segura of Colombia and Diego Palacios of Ecuador leading the way, LAFC had two of the league's most promising young defenders.

CHAPTER 4

RAISING THE BAR

Laurent Ciman waited five steps behind the ball. A wall of four Seattle Sounders defenders blocked his path 10 yards away. The 93rd-minute free kick would be LAFC's last opportunity to win its first home game. Nearby Hollywood couldn't have scripted a more dramatic ending.

At the referee's whistle, Ciman charged. With his bright red shoe, he laced a hard right-footed shot around the wall. Seattle's goalkeeper misplayed the ball and it skipped into the net. Fans in the stadium went wild. LAFC had won 1–0.

"There was a lot of excitement, and everybody felt it," Ciman said. "We really wanted to give it back to the fans."

Laurent Ciman, front, *celebrates his game-winning goal against Seattle on April 29, 2018.*

Expansion teams usually aren't very good in their early seasons. That's because they typically have to start with players that other teams didn't value highly. LAFC wasn't interested in that plan. Instead, it looked to other countries for high-priced stars such as Carlos Vela and Diego Rossi. LAFC also made smart trades for players such as defenders Ciman and Walker Zimmerman. And with a top coach in Bob Bradley leading the way, LAFC hardly looked like a first-year team.

The Black and Gold had gone on the road to Seattle and won their first game. When they beat Seattle again in their own home opener, they were 5–2–0. And the winning ways continued. LAFC never lost more than two games in a row. It reached the semifinals of the US Open Cup, a tournament for US teams at all levels. At the end of the regular season, LAFC had the third-best record in the Western Conference.

Dreams of winning an MLS Cup in their first season came crashing down in a 3–2 home loss to Real Salt Lake in the playoffs. In just one season, though, LAFC had shown it was ready to compete with the best in MLS.

BATTLE FOR LOS ANGELES

The Galaxy weren't blind to what was going on across town. For more than two decades, they had been the league's

Defender Danilo Silva, *right*, and LAFC lost a heartbreaker to Real Salt Lake in the 2018 MLS playoffs.

premier team. They'd already won a record five MLS Cups. And no team had brought more superstars into the league. Yet going into the 2018 season, the Galaxy were coming off their worst season ever. The timing of LAFC's much-hyped arrival could hardly have been worse.

Not to be upstaged, the Galaxy punched back. While Vela's arrival drew attention around MLS, the Galaxy made headlines

The first *El Tráfico* match on March 31, 2018, set the tone for a wild rivalry between the two Los Angeles MLS teams.

around the world when they signed Zlatan Ibrahimović. He was one of soccer's all-time great scorers—and characters. And he was set to make his MLS debut in the first meeting between LAFC and the Galaxy.

Their March 31 showdown proved to be one of the most anticipated regular-season MLS games ever. Soccer fans across Los Angeles had to pick their side. Did they support the established team with the global superstar? Or did they prefer the upstart team from the heart of LA, with Mexican star Vela leading the way?

Both superstars made their case in a thrilling first game. Vela scored twice early, and LAFC went up 3–0 on the road. The Black and Gold still led 3–1 when Ibrahimović was subbed on at the 71st minute. That's when everything changed. The Galaxy scored again two minutes later. Four minutes after that, Ibrahimović ripped an audacious volley from 40 yards out. It would go on to be the MLS Goal of the Year.

EL TRÁFICO

In soccer, big rivalries often have nicknames. One of the biggest rivalries in the world is *El Clásico* ("The Classic"), between Spanish powers Barcelona and Real Madrid. When LAFC met the Galaxy for the first time, fans nicknamed the game *El Tráfico* ("The Traffic"). The name was a play off El Clásico. It also poked fun at the city's famously gridlocked highways. The teams' home stadiums are just 12 miles (19 km) apart. However, in traffic that distance could feel much longer.

Then, in stoppage time, the towering Swedish striker's header gave the Galaxy the win.

It was a devastating loss for LAFC. But the game made clear that LAFC-Galaxy was MLS' hottest new rivalry. A rocking crowd came out for their second meeting that July at Banc of California Stadium. This time Vela opened the scoring as LAFC played to an exciting 2–2 draw. Both stars scored in the final meeting of 2018 the next month in Carson. Those were the only goals in a 1–1 draw.

Most neighboring sports teams are natural rivals, but the LAFC-Galaxy rivalry took that to another level, with the fans and the two superstars leading the way. With LAFC in the midst of its record-setting 2019 season, the teams met for the first time in July. Playing on the road, Vela scored twice for LAFC. However, Ibrahimović scored three times in a 3–2 win. Both again scored in their only other meeting that season, a 3–3 draw at LAFC's home field.

In just two years, the rivalry was one of the biggest stories in MLS. The games were exciting. The fans were loud. The superstars always showed up. One thing was missing, though: an LAFC win.

An LAFC supporter reminds visiting Galaxy fans they are a long way from home.

TAMING THE LION

Vela is a quiet guy. He doesn't often seek out attention. Ibrahimović is the opposite. He thrives in the biggest moments. And he seemed to delight in needling LAFC's laid-back superstar. The act helped bring lots of media attention to the rivalry. For LAFC fans, though, it was getting old. They knew the only way to shut up Ibrahimović was to finally beat him.

LAFC got that chance in the 2019 playoffs. The teams met at LAFC's home field in the quarterfinals. Many called it the most anticipated playoff game in MLS history.

An amped-up crowd of 22,902 fans awaited. Once again the teams put on a thrilling show. Vela scored twice in the first half. However, the Galaxy got one back. Then Ibrahimović tied it 2–2 early in the second. Would the Galaxy find a way to win once again?

Not this time. Vela took control of the ball in the 66th minute. He fell over. But he got back up, still in control of the ball, and found Rossi open on the wing. The Uruguayan drilled the ball into the far corner for the go-ahead goal. Then two minutes later, Rossi sent a cross to Adama Diomande, whose header made it 4–2. Although the Galaxy got one back, Diomande charged past three defenders to score again in the 80th minute. With a 5–3 win, LAFC had finally beaten the Galaxy.

Dreams of a first MLS Cup would have to wait. The Seattle Sounders upset LAFC in the Western Conference finals. The best regular season in MLS history would not end in a championship. LAFC had proven to be a force, though. That showed in 2020, when the team made the playoffs for a third straight year despite Vela missing much of the season due to injury. Fans knew that with the team's star-studded roster and aggressive front office, it was only a matter of time before the trophy cabinet began filling up.

Diego Rossi, *left*, and Jordan Harvey celebrate Rossi's goal against the Galaxy in the 2019 playoffs.

TIMELINE

2014	2015	2017	2017	2018
Chivas USA completes its final MLS season and is then disbanded. That October MLS announces Los Angeles will get a new expansion team.	The new team announces it will be called Los Angeles Football Club, or LAFC for short.	On July 27, Bob Bradley is hired to become the first LAFC head coach.	LAFC signs Mexican star Carlos Vela on August 9, making him the new team's first Designated Player.	LAFC goes on the road and defeats the Seattle Sounders 1–0 on March 4 in the team's first game.

2018	2018	2019	2019	2020
LAFC and the Galaxy meet on March 31 in the first edition of *El Tráfico*, and the Galaxy's Zlatan Ibrahimović steals the show in a 4–3 win.	In its first playoff appearance, LAFC falls 3–2 to Real Salt Lake on November 1 in the Western Conference knockout round.	Vela scores a hat trick as LAFC defeats the Colorado Rapids 3–1 in the season finale.	On October 24, LAFC finally gets past the Galaxy, beating its rivals 5–3 in a thrilling home playoff game to advance to the conference finals.	LAFC advances to the Concacaf Champions League final but falls 2–1 to Tigres UANL of Mexico.

TEAM FACTS

FIRST SEASON

2018

STADIUM

Banc of California Stadium (2018–)

SUPPORTERS' SHIELDS

2019

KEY PLAYERS

Eduard Atuesta (2018–)
Latif Blessing (2018–)
Laurent Ciman (2018)
Adama Diomande (2018–20)
Jordan Harvey (2018–)
Mark-Anthony Kaye (2018–)
Tyler Miller (2018–19)
Diego Rossi (2018–)
Eddie Segura (2019–)
Carlos Vela (2018–)
Kenneth Vermeer (2020–)
Walker Zimmerman (2018–19)

KEY COACHES

Bob Bradley (2018–)

MLS MOST VALUABLE PLAYER

Carlos Vela (2019)

MLS YOUNG PLAYER OF THE YEAR

Diego Rossi (2020)

MLS COMEBACK PLAYER OF THE YEAR

Bradley Wright-Phillips (2020)

MLS GOLDEN BOOT

Diego Rossi (2020)
Carlos Vela (2019)

MLS COACH OF THE YEAR

Bob Bradley (2019)

GLOSSARY

audacious
Bold, risky.

bicycle kick
An acrobatic strike involving a player kicking an airborne ball over his or her head back toward the goal.

cross
A pass delivered from the side of the field toward the middle.

friendlies
Soccer games that aren't part of an official league or tournament.

goal differential
The difference between the number of goals a team scores versus the number it gives up.

hat trick
Three goals by the same player in one game.

immigrants
People who move from one country to another.

salary cap
The maximum amount a team can spend on players.

stoppage time
Time added to the end of each half of a soccer game to make up for stoppages in play, such as for injuries or substitutions.

subbed on
Brought into the game as a substitute for another player who is leaving the field.

veteran
A player with a lot of experience.

volley
When a player kicks an airborne ball.

MORE INFORMATION

BOOKS

Hewson, Anthony K. *LA Galaxy.* Minneapolis, MN: Abdo Publishing, 2022.

Kortemeier, Todd. *Total Soccer.* Minneapolis, MN: Abdo Publishing, 2017.

Marthaler, Jon. *Ultimate Soccer Road Trip.* Minneapolis, MN: Abdo Publishing, 2019.

ONLINE RESOURCES

To learn more about Los Angeles Football Club, please visit **abdobooklinks.com** or scan this QR code. These links are routinely monitored and updated to provide the most current information available.

INDEX

ABOUT THE AUTHOR

Chrös McDougall is a sportswriter, editor, and children's book author. A lifelong soccer fan, he covered the opening of England's Wembley Stadium for the Associated Press and has been following Major League Soccer since the mid-2000s. McDougall lives in Minneapolis with his wife, two kids, and boxer, Eira.